**THE SEASONS**

# Winter

**BARRON'S**

It's *cold,* it's cloudy, and there is a gray wct haze that covers everything. It is the coldest season of the year and it comes after fall. Can you guess which one it is?

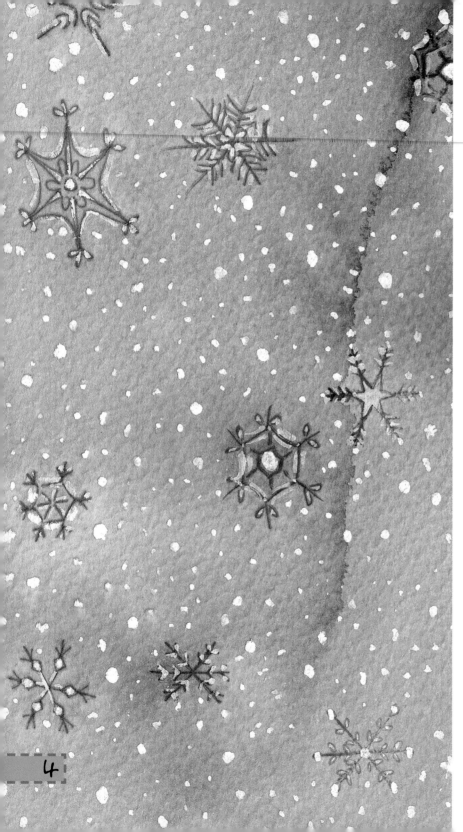

It's snowing !
In a few hours the
landscape will be all
*white.*

We can go outside
and build a
snowman. We'll have
to wear gloves,
because snow is very,
very cold !

It is so cold that water *freezes* in lakes and rivers.
Where do fish go then?
If you look carefully, maybe you'll see one!

The bear spends all winter "sleeping" in its den. This is called *hibernating*. Among the little animals on this page, three hibernate and two do not. Guess which.

hedgehog

mole

dormouse

rabbit

marmot

In the woods, birds eat the few fruits
that grow in winter, like the ones in the
*holly tree* and the *mistletoe.*
Can you find them?
Here is a clue: holly tree berries are red and
mistletoe berries are green.

How do humans manage
to spend the winter?

Surely you know three
ways to get a house warm.
Mmmm! It feels so good!

When the ground is covered in *snow,* you may go skiing or sledding. Snow is so slippery it is hard to keep your balance.

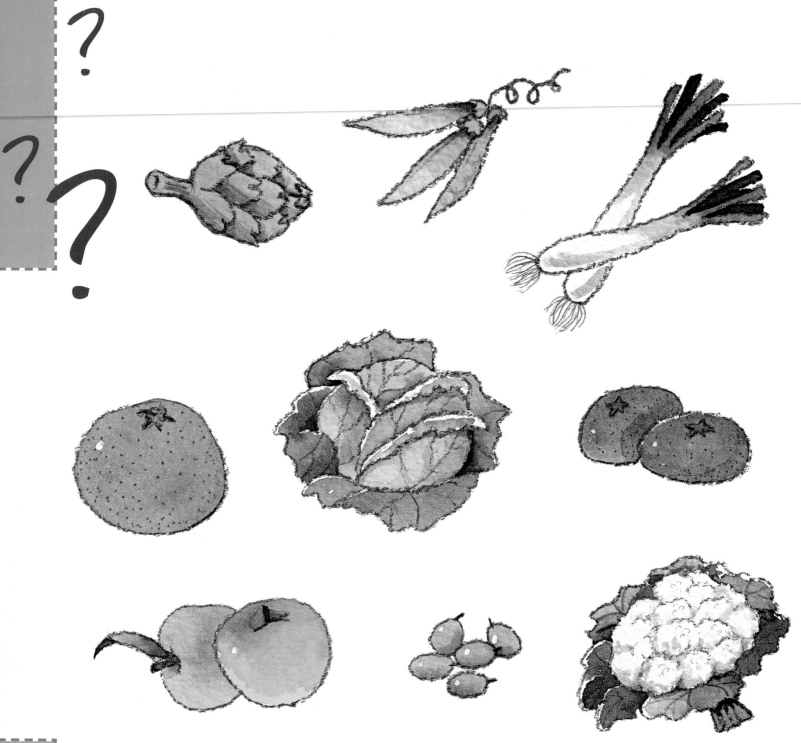

Would you like to go
to the market ? In
winter, you may find
olives, apples, leeks,
tangerines,
artichokes,
cauliflowers . . .
*and what*

In the North Pole and the South Pole it is always cold, water is extremely cold, and the land is covered in ice and _snow._ It seems like it is winter all the time!

Here you are—a lot of warm winter *clothes* so you won't be cold even if you go to the North Pole. Do you know the name of each item of clothing?

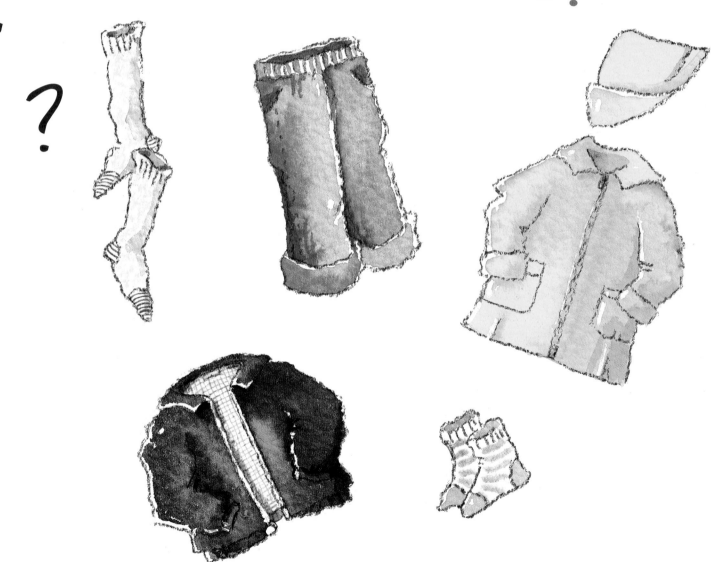

The Christmas season
is near and we
get ready to
*celebrate* it!

**Christmas** is here. Our home
is full of lights and presents !

The *end of the year* is near too. Another year is over and a new one begins. A calendar has twelve months. Do you know all of them?

Close your eyes and think what
colors remind you of winter.
White, gray, blue . . . pink?

# Illuminated greeting card

**1.** Trace the template over a piece of cardboard, paint the flame, and fold back the cardboard on both sides.

**2.** Glue the candle to another piece of cardboard of a different color and now you can finish decorating it to your taste!

# Snow stars

Now we will decorate windows with snow stars. You just need some sheets of white paper.

**1-2-3.** Fold the paper diagonally three times as shown in the instructions.

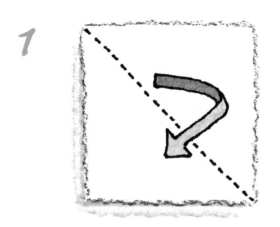

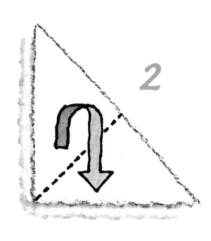

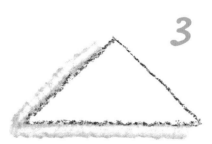

**4.** Use a pair of scissors to cut out the excess paper (the part painted blue) while copying the shape indicated in the drawing. Now you may unfold it. With a little practice, you'll be able to make lovely stars.

# Little Christmas angel

We include the templates for the body, the wings, and the head of the little angel so it will be easier for you to make it.

**1.** Trace the template for the angel's body. Cut out the figure and shape it like a cone. It will look nicer if you use a piece of colored cardboard.

**2.** Trace and cut out two wings from white, silver, or gold cardboard.

**3.** Do the same with the little angel's head.

**4.** Finally, glue the four pieces together and make a tiny hole in the star so you can thread the string through from which to hang it.

*And the little angel is ready for you to hang from your Christmas tree!*

# Let's make an Advent calendar

1. Draw the houses A and B we include here.
2. Glue house A over house B.
3. Ask a grownup to help you pierce three sides of the numbered windows with a punch.

Every day in December, as you open one of the windows,

*you will discover a nice drawing behind it.*

A

B

# Guide for the parents

## Winter has come

Winter starts on December 21st and ends on March 21st. When a new season begins, we can write down the dates of the different festivities on the calendar so children will start getting the idea of months and days. In winter it is cold, the sun rises late, and sets early, days are shorter, and nights longer. The sun is not very warm.

## Fish under the ice

When it is very cold, water freezes, which means there is a layer of ice covering the lakes. The fish in those lakes swim under the ice. When the water is extremely cold, some fish, such as pike, swim down to the bottom of the lake and stay there almost without moving. They eat practically nothing and breathe very slowly. We say they are hibernating. When the temperature gets warmer, they go back to their regular activity.

## Animals in winter

There are many ways to spend the winter. A lot of birds fly away during the winter, but some stay behind, such as blackbirds, robins, crows, starlings, titmice, magpies, and sparrows. Maybe you can spot some of them in town.

Other animals spend the winter hibernating, such as the dormouse, the woodchuck, or the badger, that comes out only once in a while to drink a little water. The mouse and the shrew make burrows between the snow and the ground so they can eat roots without having to go outside. Many other animals lead a more or less normal life and go to their dens only when weather conditions are extremely hard. This is the case of squirrels; they eat the food they stored when the weather was good. Many of these animals have more fur in winter than in summer, such as foxes.

## The Poles

Not every place on earth has the same temperature. There are places, such as the Poles, where it seems it is always winter, while at other places it is always as hot as summer, as on the equator. You can explain to older children that while it is winter in the southern hemisphere, it is summer in the northern hemisphere and vice versa. A globe and several maps are a good idea and a nice way to explain this to them.

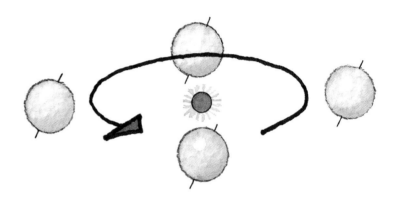

## Getting warm

We are cold in the winter because the sun does not warm us enough. We get warm using artificial heat that may come from different sources: a bonfire, Franklin stoves or gas heaters, central heating with radiators, and so on. We use water heaters so we may have hot water for our showers. We feel warm and comfortable inside our home, which is why we spend more time at home in the winter than in the summer.

## Winter colors

Every season has its own colors: cold colors and warm colors. Paint a season to teach this to your children. There is no need for a drawing first; just paint directly over the paper. Color will then be more relevant. Explain that the use of cold colors (such as violet, gray, and blue) leads to an impression of coldness, the opposite to the use of warm colors (orange, red, yellow, for instance).

Original book title in Catalan: *L'Hivern*
© Copyright Gemser Publications S.L., 2004.
C/Castell, 38; Teià (08329) Barcelona, Spain
(World Rights)
Tel: 90 540 13 63
E-mail: *info@mercedesros.com*
Author: Núria Roca
Illustrator: Rosa Maria Curto

First edition for the United States and Canada
(exclusive rights), and the rest of the world (non-
exclusive rights) published in 2004 by Barron's
Educational Series, Inc.

*Address all inquiries to:*
Barron's Educational Series, Inc.
250 Wireless Boulevard
Hauppauge, New York 11788
**http://www.barronseduc.com**

ISBN-13: 978-0-7641-2731-1
ISBN-10: 0-7641-2731-4
Library of Congress Catalog Card Number 2004101342

Printed in China
9 8 7 6 5 4 3

THE SEASONS

Winter